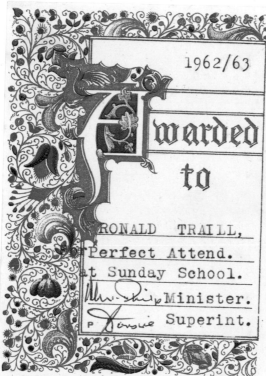

1962/63

Awarded to

RONALD TRAILL,

Perfect Attend.

t Sunday School.

_____ Minister.

P _____ Superint.

Church of Scotland Bookshop, 125A Nethergate, Dundee.

Michael and Rosemary climbed a few feet higher

page 2

THE YOUNG EXPLORERS

by

LYDIA S. ELIOTT

LUTTERWORTH PRESS
LONDON

First printed 1958
Reprinted 1959

COPYRIGHT © LUTTERWORTH PRESS 1958

PRINTED IN GREAT BRITAIN BY
EBENEZER BAYLIS AND SON, LIMITED, THE
TRINITY PRESS, WORCESTER, AND LONDON

CONTENTS

Chapter One

SECRET SURPRISE

"IT would be terrific to be an explorer like Livingstone, wouldn't it?" Michael remarked to his sister Rosemary, as they came skipping along on their way home from Sunday School.

"Yes, I'd love it," Rosemary agreed, "except I'd be afraid of lions. I'd like to go where there *aren't* lions, but I suppose it wouldn't be valiant." Rosemary began singing the Pilgrim Hymn, "He who would valiant be, Let him come hither." Sunday School had ended with that hymn; it was both Michael's and Rosemary's favourite.

Michael broke into a run as they reached the road where they lived. "Come along, Rosemary. Aren't you aching to hear what Dad's secret surprise is?"

"Yes, I am, but it won't be quite tea-time when we get in, and Dad said he'd tell us at tea-time, not before."

"Oh, bother! So he did." Michael slowed back to a walk as he spoke. "Whatever can the surprise be? Mum doesn't like us to ask questions about it, but she's answered a few, and it doesn't seem to be anything ordinary . . . not holidays, or an outing or a treat."

"Wouldn't it be lovely if we were going to be explorers!"

"Well, we won't be, you little dafty." Michael did not speak unkindly. The two children were good friends and quarrelled very seldom. There was only a year between them, but Rosemary was tall for her age and so they were just the same height. People sometimes took them for twins, though they were not alike to look at. Michael was fair and round, and Rosemary dark-haired and blue-eyed like her father.

"Mum, is it nearly tea-time?" Michael asked, rushing into the house like a whirlwind, and then on into the kitchen where he found his mother.

"No, dear," Mrs. Lansdowne answered. "Dad won't be in for half an hour or so. He has gone round to see Granny."

"Oh! dear, did he *have* to go? He promised he'd tell us the secret surprise at tea-time." Michael forgot all his good intentions, stamped his foot and looked downright cross.

"Now, Michael, look cheerful. You know Dad will keep his promise. Granny wanted to see him specially and she comes first. You must try to be patient. You have been much better lately. I know you have tried."

Rosemary came into the kitchen as Mrs. Lansdowne was speaking.

"Well, chicks," their mummy said, "tell me about Sunday School." Michael's ill-temper vanished as he began telling the story of Livingstone.

"We'd love to be explorers like Livingstone, Rosemary and me, but Rosemary doesn't want to go where there are lions. I should like lions. It would be thrilling, having adventures."

"But he didn't just have adventures, Miss Lovelle told us," Rosemary joined in. "He made people well and taught them about Jesus. She said we mustn't forget that Livingstone didn't go there to *have* adventures—they happened."

"He did have them though," Michael declared.

"Awfully exciting ones, and he did explore, and find out about Africa things no one knew before. I'm going to be an explorer when I grow up. I want to be one more than——" but Michael did not finish for he heard Dad's key in the front door.

He jumped round his father and took a little case from him that he was carrying.

"Dad, is the surprise in here?"

"Well, yes, there's a good deal about it. I've been showing it to Granny. Put it on my desk please, Michael," his father said.

Both children watched their father anxiously as he sat down to tea. At last he had his cup in his hand. He really had begun.

"Very good scones and toasted just right," he remarked in an ordinary voice, pretending not to see how excited the children were.

"Oh, Dad, you *are* a tease!" Michael burst out.

Rosemary looked imploringly at her mother. Mrs. Lansdowne understood her look.

"Yes, dear, I think Dad is ready now."

Mr. Lansdowne smiled at his wife and children, his eyes sparkling with fun. He was enjoying the children's eagerness.

"Well, my dears," he said slowly.

"Oh! Dad, do be quick and tell us," Rosemary begged.

"We are off to Canada three weeks tomorrow!"

For a moment the children stared blankly, then gasped, "Canada, going to Canada!"

"But, Dad, we can't. School will have started. There's only a week and a bit of holidays left now!" Rosemary exclaimed.

"Yes, I know that, but you won't be at school.

You'll be boarding a big liner at the docks." He looked at his watch. "No, we ought to have left the docks by now. It's five o'clock, we should be going down towards the Needles."

"Dad, you're not just joking, are you? Do you really mean that we are all going to Canada?" Michael stammered with excitement. Then, leaving his scone half-eaten, he went and stood by his father's chair.

"When shall we come back?" Rosemary asked anxiously. "Will we have a long holiday in Canada? Why are we going? Why didn't we go at the beginning of the holidays?"

"What boat are we going on, Dad?" Michael asked. "May I go to the engine-room and see things? Will there be a swimming pool? How will they do without you at the office? Who will look after the chickens while we're away?"

And the two might have gone on asking question after question had not their parents laughed at them. "Do stop asking Dad questions, children," their mother begged. "You're not giving him a chance to tell us more about the surprise. I want to hear lots more."

Michael went back to his seat and both children were silent at last.

"Now I can explain a bit," Mr. Lansdowne began. "You know that we get a great deal of the timber which you have seen in the timber-yards from Canada, most of it from the far west in British Columbia, and when it is unloaded at the docks here I examine it and make sure that it is all right and write lists of it. Then I help to get it sent off to the people who have ordered it. Well, Mr. Watson, he is head of the firm, has asked me to go to British Columbia, right on the far side of Canada, six thousand miles away, to the firm's office there. He wants me to examine the timber that we buy there and get it sent off to Southampton."

Mr. Lansdowne paused to get on with his tea. He had given the children plenty to think about.

"It's very serious, isn't it? It's not a bit the kind of surprise I thought it would be." Rosemary sounded so solemn that her parents and Michael laughed and then she joined in.

"Yes, dear, it is serious," Mr. Lansdowne said gently. "Your mother and I have thought a great deal about whether we ought to go or not, and we have prayed about it, and now we feel sure that God wants us to leave our home here, and take you to Canada and make a new home there, and that He will bless and help us."

"I think it's gorgeous, spiffling, wizard! I don't mind leaving home a bit," Michael declared. "I do love new things. Don't you *want* to go, Dad? Don't you *want* to, Mum?"

"Yes, I want to," his father replied, "but your Mummy will be sad to leave her mother and sister, and she will have hard work starting a new home. Both of you will try to help her, I know, and try not to do things that make her anxious."

"I don't know if I want to go," Rosemary looked up at her mother. "I don't want to leave the garden and school and Jean." Jean was one of Rosemary's friends.

"You *are* unsporting, Rosemary," Michael spoke scornfully.

"Now, Michael, don't be so hasty. There's a lot to be sorry about, in leaving our old home and our friends. But Canada is a fine country for boys and girls to grow up in. There are good schools and colleges and you'll have a healthy outdoor life."

"Can we be real explorers, Dad?" Michael had not been listening to what his father said last, for he was impatient to hear more about where they were going. Now he did not wait for his father to reply. "Rosemary, you'll explore with me, won't you? We'll start an exploring gang."

"Steady on, Michael," his father said, smiling at him. "You'll have to go a bit slow. Your cousins there and other children will know about everything much better than you. You must not try to boss or you'll be unhappy. We'll all have to be patient and explore new ways of doing things and try to fit in. There will be plenty of exploring to do, but not quite the sort you mean."

Michael fell silent. He did love bossing. He began to wonder if he really wanted to leave his school in Southampton.

"It'll be more like being pilgrims than explorers, won't it?" Rosemary spoke thoughtfully. "We've had the Pilgrim Hymn at Sunday School this afternoon, Dad."

"Yes, you're right, child. Now let's get tea cleared away and the washing-up done, then I'll explain from a big map just where we are going."

A little later Mrs. Lansdowne and the children were looking eagerly at the map while Mr. Lansdowne traced their journey.

"This is where we are now, see?" Mr. Lansdowne pointed to Southampton. The Lansdownes lived a little way out of the town. With a pencil he followed a dotted line that crossed the Atlantic. "This is the course the steamer will follow. It will take us seven days in the *Honora* to cross the ocean. She's not a fast boat but very comfortable. Then we shall sail up the St. Lawrence River." He pointed out the river. "Past Quebec, and land at Montreal. We shall stay one night there, and then go on by a great big train right across Canada."

"How long does the train take?" asked Michael, jumping up and down with excitement.

"Five days and five nights."

"Shall we have beds in the train?" Rosemary asked. "We couldn't stay awake all the time, could we?"

"Yes, we shall have beds. Berths, they call them. You and Michael may have the top ones if you like—it's rather fun climbing up with a ladder—and Mummy and I will have the two under you. They are booked ready for us. We shall get off the train here at Vancouver City, and then go by steamer across the sea between the mainland and Vancouver Island. Do you see the island? It's big, and there's Victoria at the south of it."

"Are we really going to live there, in Victoria?" Rosemary put her finger on the town. "Is it a real, proper seaside place?"

"Yes, there is sea nearly all round where we shall live."

"It'll be great telling the chaps at school about it!" exclaimed Michael. "They've never been on a journey like ours will be, I'm sure."

"You will not be going to school here any more. There will only be ten days of the summer term before we sail. The heads of your schools know that you are leaving, and Mr. Roberts would like Michael to go and say good-bye to him the day before school begins, and Miss Enfield will be coming to tea with Mummy one day next week and you would like to be in and see her and say good-bye, I know, Rosemary."

Mr. Lansdowne was quite glad that Michael would not get much chance of boasting. Of course they would ask two or three of his special friends to come to tea, or perhaps to an outing. It would have been hard for any boy not to be a bit boastful about their journey and about the lovely place where they were to live, and the exciting things there would be to do.

When their father had told them more about Victoria it was still light enough for the children to go into the garden to let off steam for a while before they had the Sunday evening hymn singing which they loved, and the time when Dad and Mum would tell them a Sunday story.

"May we sing the Pilgrim Hymn first, since we're going to be pilgrims?" Rosemary asked when their mother was seated at the piano.

Michael went to the bookcase and brought *The Pilgrim's Progress* to the table when they had sung the hymn.

"Mum, find our hymn in the book, please!" Mrs. Lansdowne found the place and the children looked at the pictures beside it.

"That's a lovely hobgoblin, isn't it?" Michael pointed to a creature like a dragon with a snake's head and wings, and claws, and a very curly tail.

"There's a lion too," said Rosemary, "but he's not clear. Perhaps he's far away; and there are snakes. Are they foul fiends, Dad?"

"Do you remember a picture of two other lions?" Dad asked them. "Timid and Notrust, though they were God's pilgrims, turned back when they saw them by the side of the path. Here's the picture. They forgot to trust to God to take care of them."

"How awfully angry they look!" exclaimed Rosemary. "But I remember the story now. Christian didn't turn back, because Watchful called to him, 'Fear not the lions, God has chained them.' Christian couldn't see the chains, could he? But look, they do show in the picture if you look close."

"What do the lions mean for us?" their mother asked.

"I'm afraid of lots of things," Rosemary spoke shyly. "New people and the dark and being alone and . . ."

"You will try not to be afraid, won't you, dear? God won't let any lions hurt you, if you trust Him."

"I'm not afraid of anything!" declared Michael, standing up and pretending to fight.

"Aren't you?" asked his father, smiling. "I think you are. I think you're afraid of what other boys say, sometimes. You don't like to be called unsporting. The Pilgrim Hymn says, 'I'll fear not what men say' . . . It's very hard, you know, even for grown-ups."

"I don't care what boys say," Michael repeated.

"He's like Mr. Boastful, isn't he?" said Rosemary, and they all laughed and Michael managed to laugh too. "You're a bit like Miss Much-afraid, Rosemary." But Michael did not speak unkindly.

"There's just time for one more hymn and then bed," Mrs. Lansdowne said.

"I'd like 'Jesus I have promised to serve thee to the end'," said Michael. "And *I* want to have 'Abide with me'," said Rosemary. "It is so peace-ifying to go to go to bed on."

"Well, we will have the first two verses of 'O Jesus I have promised', and we will have the first and fourth verses of 'Abide with me'."

The children as well as their parents were still and silent after the words, "Through cloud and sunshine, O abide with me!" They felt that God was near them, and blessing them all.

"What a lovely Sunday evening," Rosemary spoke

gently. "It's been very special—the surprise, and then starting to be pilgrim-explorers, and the hymns."

Even Michael undressed and prepared for bed without chattering all the time as he usually did. The hymns were still singing themselves in his heart.

Chapter Two

AN EXCITING JOURNEY

FOR the last five days in England the family stayed with the children's grandmother and aunt in Southampton. It seemed as if these days would never end. Michael could not settle to anything. He was cock-a-hoop every moment, rushing from one room to another, trying to turn cartwheels in the garden, and describing the wonderful things that he was going to do in Canada, till his father called him "Mr. Boastful" and when he boasted again said, "Why, Mr. Boastful is with us still. I hoped he had gone away."

Michael had no regrets at leaving England, nor had his father. For several years he had been hoping that he would be asked to go to the firm's offices in British Columbia. It would be a grand life for the children on Vancouver Island, though his wife was not altogether happy about going.

It was on the last evening when the children were in bed and asleep and the grown-ups were having a talk that she explained what was worrying her.

"I know," she said, "it will be a splendid life for the children and I know the schools are good, and it will cost less when they leave school to train them for what they want to do, but I am afraid of accidents. Michael is so rash and venturesome, and Rosemary always does what he wants them to do, even if she is frightened, and with sea and cliffs close to our home, I can't help being anxious."

"Their cousins will look after them at first, I'm sure,"

the children's grandmother said. "Your house will only be half a mile or so away from theirs. Anne's fifteen now and Geoff fourteen. They will see that Michael and Rosemary do not come to any harm."

"Yes, I suppose they will, but that worries me, too. You see, Michael doesn't like anyone looking after him, and they can both be pretty stubborn, bless them," and Mrs. Lansdowne laughed. She felt happier now that they had talked over her anxieties. "I mustn't be a fussy mother," she thought to herself, and, "I must be more trustful. God will take care of them, and help me to be wise."

So on the day of sailing, all the family were looking forward to the new life and to the exciting journey.

"I wish *we* were coming," their grandmother told the children. "You're very lucky youngsters."

The very air quivered with excitement as Michael, Rosemary, their parents, grandmother and aunt climbed up the gangway on to the *Honora*. They were not the only excited people. Crowds bustled about, passengers and friends who were seeing them off, telegraph boys, errand boys with armfuls of flowers, stewards showing people to their cabins, and children running hither and thither in their eagerness to explore the ship, jostled each other good-temperedly.

At last came the shout, "All visitors ashore", and the stewards hurried round the ship determined that there should be no stowaways. The children's grandmother and aunt stood on the quay waving as the bugler played the boat off. The sound of the bugle, announcing that the moment for leaving England had really come, made Rosemary feel like crying. She couldn't think why, for she was happy. She blinked back the tears that came to her eyes and waved again to her granny. "God bless you, darling, and take care of Mummy for me," her granny had said, as she kissed her a few minutes before. "It is lovely of Granny to trust me with taking care of Mummy, and God will help me to. It's part of being a pilgrim," she thought.

Everyone was excited as the ship quivered through her whole frame. Then the little tugs pulled the great lines off and the strip of water widened between the quay and the ship. There was no going back now. "First stop Quebec," said the indicator on the deck.

An exploration tour round the boat was conducted for all the boys and girls who cared to go. Jimmy, the steward who looked after the gymnasium, took them to the swimming bath, the library, the gymnasium, and other parts of the ship which he thought would interest them. When the party was growing tired, it was tea time, with cream buns and eclairs. After tea, eaten in the children's dining-room, Michael and Rosemary found that their mother had unpacked all that they would need for the voyage. They loved their four-berth cabin, and their father let them climb up and down the ladder to the top berths as often as they liked, for they were still in the calm waters of the Solent.

The *Honora* had an unusually warm, sunny crossing of the Atlantic for May. The children had breakfast and the midday meal with their parents in the dining saloon where the grown-ups had meals. They enjoyed this. One morning at breakfast Michael grumbled because the weather was so sunny and calm.

"I wish we could have a big storm! No, I shouldn't be ill. I'd stand on the top deck and watch the waves crashing over us. Oh, it would be fun, and I should be so brave."

"I'd hate it," said Rosemary. "It's horrid when there's

a noise, and I might be sea-sick, and you might be too, Michael. You don't know you wouldn't be, for you've never tried, and they'd not let you stand on the top deck. They put canvas all round the decks when there's a storm and you have to keep to the lower decks. Jimmy told me all about it."

"You're just being Miss Much-Afraid."

"I'm not! But you're worse than Mr. Boastful. You're horrid." Rosemary and Michael were starting one of their rare quarrels.

"Now, children, you're both over-excited. There's nothing to quarrel about. Remember you are pilgrims, and pilgrims are being bad ones if they quarrel."

"But the crusaders quarrelled awfully," broke in Michael.

"Yes, they did," Mr. Lansdowne agreed. "And when they quarrelled they were not God's pilgrims any longer. They were selfish, boastful people."

There was a shamefaced silence, and soon the quarrel was forgotten.

Mr. and Mrs. Lansdowne were very thankful that the crossing had been calm and sunny. On the last evening before they docked there was a service in the library for the passengers who cared to attend. The minister who was taking it had made friends with Michael and Rosemary and half a dozen other children, so that they were keen to go to the Service. He spoke to all the children for a few minutes.

"I want you to think of all the happy and beautiful things that have come to you on the voyage and of all the people who have been kind to you and taken care of you. Then we will thank God for these blessings and ask Him to show us how we can make other people happy in the new life that most of you are going to start in Canada. God will never forget any one of you and I want you never to forget Him. His love is always round about you."

At ten o'clock the next night the boat neared Montreal. The children were tired and sleepy and their parents wanted to pass through the Customs quickly so that the children could get to bed and to sleep in the hotel where they were staying for one night.

Suddenly everyone forgot their tiredness, for all the fairy lights on every deck of the *Honora* were switched on, and the ship was ablaze with rainbow lighting, throwing red, green and gold dapplings on the dark waters beneath. They were still delighting in this surprise when flood-lighting was switched on over the docks to greet them.

Rosemary declared that she enjoyed the five days' journey on the big, snorting train more than the voyage. Though the ocean was such glorious colours and always changing, it was nothing but sea everywhere, but as the train "moo-ed" its way across Canada from east to west, there was always something quite new to see. At first they did not like the funny snorting, mooing sound that the great engine made to warn people and animals to keep off the unfenced railway lines. It went on day and night, but soon they grew fond of it. It gave them a warm, friendly feeling.

Birds, forests, lakes, Indian tepees, the prairies, and then the massive snow-topped mountains of the Rockies with their rushing torrents and gay flowers, gave the children something new to see and to talk of every day. They both liked to spend much time on the open-air platform at the end of the train. Here they were so near the animals and flowers and the rushing torrents.

When the children were not on the open-air platform, watching the railway lines gliding away mile after mile behind then and sometimes seeing a buffalo, or a bear newly out of his winter den, lumbering away from the train, they spent the time in the armchair car where there were magazines and books and the radio, except after the evening meal when they and their parents sat in their own little compartment in the big sleeping-car. There were four seats here, two and two facing each other. About eight o'clock this compartment was turned into four berths, but in the half hour before the attendant made their beds, the family met and talked over the day and all they had seen.

Both Michael and Rosemary were almost dazed with the many new and wonderful things they saw each day. Mr. Lansdowne read them parts of the poem *Hiawatha* as they travelled through the country of the great lakes. There they saw the murmuring pines and the hemlocks, and the lakes and rushing rivers.

One night as soon as it was dark an electric storm lit up the prairies. It may have been far away, but the lightning flashed rose, lilac, gold, blue and delicate green, colouring the northern sky for an hour or more. Rosemary was naturally afraid of thunder storms, but her mother drew up the blind close to her berth and she lay and watched the ever-changing colours happily. It was so beautiful that fear left her, and she repeated to herself:

> "All things bright and beautiful
> All creatures great and small
> All things wise and wonderful
> The Lord God made them all.

As they crossed Canada both children began to feel

in a new way that the world was God's world and that He had made it full of beautiful and wonderful things that they had never known existed before.

After three days the train began to climb the eastern slopes of the Rocky Mountains, and one morning directly after breakfast the train stopped at a halt high up in the foothills where there was still snow left, and the conductor of each coach put steps to the doors and helped all the passengers out who wanted to go exploring or to have a walk.

"Now, ladies and gentlemen," he warned them, "you must be back in an hour. You must not be one minute late or the train will leave you behind."

Chapter Three

TREED BY A BEAR

DURING the three-day journey Michael and Rosemary had made friends with a Mr. Richards and his friend Mr. Giles. Like the children they often spent time on the observation platform watching the animals. Mr. Richards had told the children about the great herds of buffalo which used to roam on the prairies and had made sure that they saw the herd which lives in a reserve bordering the railway. Then he had told them to look out for deer, and since reaching the forests they had seen a number of large deer and smaller deer with their young fawns.

"We shall see bears," he told them. "The brown and black bears are just out of their dens now with their young cubs. It's not likely that we shall see grizzlies until we are running down the western slopes of the Rockies."

Rosemary was never tired of hearing about animals.

"You'll see all kinds of deer, bears, beavers and mountain lions on Vancouver Island, a little north of Victoria," he said. "But when they give us an hour out of the train on the mountains, Mr. Giles and I are going to try to get photographs of bears."

So Mr. Richards and Mr. Giles took their movie cameras and Michael and Rosemary were excited to be going with them. They went round behind the big hotel which was almost the only building near the halt, to the open space on the edge of the forest where there were a number of hotel rubbish bins. Mr. Richards knew that bears often came there to hunt for sweet things and sometimes they brought their cubs. He had been lucky in getting photographs there before.

The photographers were excited and everyone had a happy, thrilled feeling: it was partly the mountain air and partly being out of the train after three days of living in it. Michael and Rosemary had never had such a don't-care-what-happens feeling in their lives before, or such longing for adventure. If their parents had realized this, they would not have let them go off alone with the photographers!

Mr. Richards, Mr. Giles and the children had not long to wait, for a big black bear plodded out of the forest behind them, put his head and shoulders right into a rubbish bin to seize a partly empty treacle tin, and then fell in head foremost and could not get out. How the photographers and the children laughed! And the bear looked funnier still when he rolled the bin on its side on the ground and rolled with it until he could free his head and shoulders. The photographers thought that they had got one of the most wonderful films that they had ever secured.

In a few minutes the bear went away carrying the partly empty treacle tin with him. The photographers were sure more bears would come and were keen to get other photographs. After a few minutes Michael and Rosemary grew bored, and started to explore in the forest. At first they were not out of sight of the photographers, but when they had scrambled in a little way between trees and over rocks, they came to a grassy path. It was easy going along this, and they were soon out of sight and hearing of the others.

It was not until a big mother bear lumbered out of the trees and stood about twelve yards away growling at them that they remembered that they had promised not to leave the photographers. Michael would have turned and run back the way they had come, but Rosemary put out her hand and stopped him. Mr. Richards had told her that you must never run away from bears, or they will chase you and catch up with you and maul you. If you don't run away from them, and if they have not got young cubs, black and brown bears will not touch you, though grizzlies are always dangerous.

The two stood where they were and the mother bear stood growling. Her little beady eyes glared with anger, and in less than a minute the children saw the reason: a tiny cub wobbled out of the trees and stood beside her. She took a step forward and growled again.

"She can't climb," whispered Rosemary, and as quickly as possible Michael and she were ten feet up a tree that had low branches. The bear came on and the cub rolled along behind her.

Michael and Rosemary climbed a few feet higher, reaching a fork between a strong branch and the trunk of the tree and wedging themselves there. They clung on too with their hands. The bear reached the tree, reared up on her hind legs and clawed at the trunk, trying to shake the children down, but Michael and Rosemary had lots of pluck and clung on. The mother-bear growled up at them, showing her teeth in a frightening snarl. She was angry. Why should these children come into the forest threatening her baby? She would take care that they did not get it. She lowered her massive body and sat down, back to the tree, leaning against it and drawing the cub to her with an arm round it.

If only the photographers had remembered the children and come to look for them!

"What shall we do if she stays here?" Rosemary whispered. It would have made no difference if she had spoken aloud, the bear was paying no attention to them. She was murmuring gently to the cub. The Scandinavians say that a bear is as clever as twelve men. This mother bear was certainly very clever. She had treed Michael and Rosemary and meant to keep them treed as long as she wished. They had to be back at the train at half-past ten. Michael's watch showed that it was ten already. Fear seized them both. She might keep them there hours! It would take them ten minutes, in any case, to run back to the train.

"Oh, Michael, what shall we do? What can we do?" Rosemary was terribly distressed.

"Shout! We must shout our loudest. Some of the passengers must hear us."

They shouted until they were breathless and hoarse, but there was no sound in reply.

"We'll have to try and make a dash for it," Michael declared. "There's only a quarter of an hour left. We'll climb down the tree on the side away from the bear and run."

"It'll be awfully dangerous," Rosemary told him. "I think Mum and Dad would rather we missed the train than were killed!"

But Michael was determined to try. They had only just begun to move from the fork where they had been sitting wedged together when the bear let go of her cub and reared up the tree again, tearing the bark of the tree into shreds and growling fiercely. She tried to shake the children down, but the tree was too big and strong.

"We can't risk it," Rosemary gasped, "she'd tear us to pieces. We must ask God to take care of us and help us, though we've done what we oughtn't to."

They were both praying in their hearts. They hardly
dared to look at the time—only ten minutes now till the
train would leave. Would anyone find out that they
weren't on it? Would the photographers remember
them? Perhaps their parents would think they were on
the open platform at the back of the train. Perhaps they
wouldn't keep the train even if they found out the
children were missing. "But Mum and Dad would stay
behind," Michael groaned, "if they knew."

When there were only five minutes left, a new idea
came into the bear's head, for pushing her cub on
in front of her she ambled off towards the hotel dust-
bins. Michael and Rosemary climbed noiselessly down
to the ground and ran as fast as they could, but part of
the way was through thick undergrowth. They reached
the railway to see the rear of the train gliding out of
sight round a bend on the line.

There was no one at all about. The only porter had
gone off on the train itself to the next halt, as there
would not be another train for twelve hours.

"They think we're on the train," gasped Michael, as
soon as he had breath enough to speak.

"How awful! What *shall* we do?" Rosemary was
struggling to keep back tears. "I thought they'd find
out we weren't on the train, and we *were* nearly in time."

"Mr. Richards ought to have looked for us. I know
we ought not to have gone away from him, but . . ."
Then Michael pulled himself together. "We must do
something. The hotel is the only place we can go. We
must ask them to help us."

"Yes, we must," Rosemary agreed, though she felt
terrified of going to the large, grand hotel.

They hurried back, but it needed all their courage to
go up the drive to the hotel. A big shining car was drawn

up at the elegant entrance doors, and a big man was calling orders to a group round him. Michael and Rosemary saw that he was angry. He looked very frightening.

"Disgraceful," he shouted, "having that clock a quarter of an hour slow and letting me miss the train. Disgraceful, I tell you. Now you get a message to the next halt. Contact the flag-man. He *must* flag the train, and it must wait for me. Understand? See you make *them* understand."

Michael and Rosemary felt as if he were angry with them, as soon he was. He waved them away. "Take those dirty children away," he ordered. They certainly did look dirty! Their faces and clothes were smudged with lichen and moss.

"Come, children," said a hall porter, but Michael and Rosemary held their ground, and Michael, taking Rosemary's hand, pulled her along till the two of them were standing against the car door so that Major Greatrex, for that was his name, could not get in.

"What's this?" he said crossly, but as he looked at the children and saw how miserable and anxious they were, his face softened. He was very fond of children.

"What are you two doing?" he asked.

"Please," began Michael, "we've missed that train. Mum and Dad are on it. They think we're on it too."

"It's *awful*," Rosemary blurted out. "Please take us with you!"

To the amazement of the men whom he had been scolding, Major Greatrex opened the back door of the car.

"Tumble in," he ordered the children and slammed the door and then sprang into the front. "We'll do it," he said over his shoulder to comfort them. "I'll take care of you." His ill-temper had vanished. He'd see they got into the train. It was not a race just on his own account now; he couldn't leave these two kids behind in the middle of nowhere.

After forty minutes they caught sight of the train. "We're beating it!" Major Greatrex was jubilant. "We'll be there ourselves to see that the train is flagged," and they were.

The drivers and guards of the important Trans-Continental Express were both surprised and annoyed to find the train had been flagged to stop at a halt where they never stopped unless there was something wrong with the train, and nothing *was* wrong. She was running splendidly and up to time. This stop would make her late.

Michael and Rosemary watched the huge express thunder out of a tunnel, screaming as it came. Would it stop? Would they really get back aboard to their parents? Was it stopping? It hardly seemed to be slowing down at all.

"It *is* stopping!" shouted Rosemary, jumping up and down. "It's going to stop."

"Of course it is, child." Major Greatrex was amused at her.

The train drew up for one minute only. One of the conductors on the train flung open a door close to where Major Greatrex and the children were standing. The Major lifted up Rosemary and then Michael and then sprang aboard himself, and the train was away again so quickly that only a very few passengers knew why the train was stopped, or had seen Major Greatrex and the children.

Mr. and Mrs. Lansdowne had only discovered ten minutes before the train stopped that Michael and Rosemary were missing. They were horrified. The guard had just told them that the train was flagged to stop at the next halt and that he could put them off if they liked. While they were in a panic of misery and doubt as to whether to get off or not the children were miraculously returned to them.

"Please, please, do forgive us," they both begged. "We didn't mean not to keep near Mr. Richards. We meant to go back to him, but we were treed by a bear!"

When Rosemary saw that their parents still looked both grieved and severe, she asked, "Please, you'd rather we'd missed the train than were killed, wouldn't you? We really thought you'd rather we waited. We really did."

"Of course it was right to wait, but you ought not to have left Mr. Richards and Mr. Giles and gone into the forest," Mr. Lansdowne said, with the crossness of relief. "Then you wouldn't have been treed by the bear. You have distressed your mother very badly, and the worst is that we can't trust you to be sensible."

"We do mind awfully, worrying you and Mummy," Rosemary said, "and being such bad pilgrims. What can we do to make up?"

"There's one thing you can do. Remember that you are not in this world to please yourselves. Even Jesus did not please himself. Try to think of other people first, and God will help you to follow the Master, just as our Pilgrim Hymn says."

Michael and Rosemary sat silent, very sad when they realized how selfish they had been and how badly they had troubled their parents.

"Well, it's all over now," Mr. Lansdowne said cheerfully, "over and done with, and now we'll play Snakes and Ladders to cheer ourselves up."

Chapter Four

A NEW HOME

As it was Friday evening when the Trans-Continental reached Vancouver City, the Lansdownes stayed there till Monday morning. They spent Saturday afternoon on a sandy beach in West Vancouver. How Michael and Rosemary delighted in the sea, and in the trees leaning over the beach up which they could climb, and sit perched with the waves beneath them!

"Will it be like this on Vancouver Island near our house?" asked Rosemary. "Will it be as lovely?"

"It'll be as lovely, I'm sure," her father replied, "but we don't know if there'll be trees to climb."

All the family were glad of a quiet day on Sunday. They had enjoyed the voyage and the long train journey, but seeing so many new things is tiring. They went to church in the morning. The minister spoke for a few minutes to the boys and girls before giving a sermon to the grown-ups. He spoke of the love and care that parents give their boys and girls, and that the best way to show thankfulness is for them to show love and care for their parents by not doing things that worry them. Jesus said that we are loving God when we love those around us and make them happy.

"Are people happier because you are at home?" he asked the children, "or are you like a girl of whom I was told: everyone dreaded her coming home from boarding-school for holidays, she was unhappy, and she spread gloom round her. Do you bring happiness or anxiety into your home?"

Rosemary and Michael blushed, thinking of the bear. They asked God to help them to be bringers of happiness.

The last hour of the five-hour voyage from Vancouver City to Victoria on the southern tip of Vancouver Island had come. The boat was threading its way between tiny islands crowned with pine trees and girdled with beaches of golden sand.

"What lovely places to bathe!" exclaimed Michael, as the family were gazing in wonder at the islands and shining blue sea from the deck. "Shall we be able to come here and bathe?"

"There will be sandy bays much nearer our house," his father told him.

At last the first houses of Victoria were in sight. They stood a little above the sea among trees, their gay gardens sloping to the water's edge, each with its private sandy cove.

"Will our house be like those?" asked Rosemary. "Will it have a private beach? Can we bathe this evening, if it has?" She paused to take breath, unintentionally giving her father a chance to answer her questions.

"Our house will not be as big as those and I don't think that it will have a private bathing beach, though I'm sure it will be quite near the sea."

Silence fell on the little group as they watched the cliffs, golden with broom, slide past them, and gazed at the sparkling blue water. They could hardly believe that it was true that they were to live near this beautiful city set upon the sea. The clear afternoon sunshine was dimpling the sparkling blue water with gold and lighting up the flowers in the brilliant gardens of the Parliament buildings as their boat drew alongside the quay.

The first person they saw on shore was Mrs. Lansdowne's brother Mr. Johnson, the children's Uncle Fred. They had heard lots about him and he had sent them Christmas presents. He was like Mrs. Lansdowne, except that he was taller and broader, and he had the same smile, a smile that made children take to him at once.

"This is great!" he exclaimed. "You're here at last. My whole family has come to meet you. We've brought two cars. We'll collect your luggage in a few minutes, but come along first and meet each other."

A charming lady who was sitting in the driver's seat of the first car was the children's Aunt Susan.

"This is Anne, our eldest," said Uncle Fred.

"How pretty she is," Rosemary thought, as Anne smiled at her and helped her into the first car, and then sat beside her.

Soon the luggage was all stacked in the cars and off they drove, first through the city, and then along a wide tree-bordered road straight out to the coast.

"We are going to our house first to have tea," Anne explained to Rosemary. "It's on the way to yours."

"Is it like ours? Is it close to the sea?" Rosemary checked herself. "I'm sorry. I'm awful at asking questions. I don't give people time to answer."

Anne laughed. She thought Rosemary amusing. "Perhaps we needn't mind the Lansdownes coming after all," she said to herself. "They don't seem so bad as I thought they'd be." Anne and Geoff had not liked the idea of these English cousins: they seemed to give so much trouble, their dad having to find a house for them and their mother having to get it ready, and Anne had had to help. But they had promised to try their best— and, after all, they thought, Michael and Rosemary might be some good for games and sailing.

The cars had just turned west along a road with houses on one side and the sea on the other when Aunt Susan drew up outside a white one-storey house with a green shingled roof. The front door was reached by a flight of wide steps. Underneath the house were the garage and the basement where wood was stored and where there was a furnace used for heating the house in winter. The front door opened into a spacious glassed veranda. The windows were thrown wide on this hot June day and in a few minutes Anne and Geoff had carried out all that was needed for tea.

"This is a wonderful spot! What a view!" exclaimed Mrs. Lansdowne.

From where the party was sitting at tea, they looked across the garden and the road to the sea. The sands were hidden, because there was a drop from the road of ten feet or so and the tide was in. Thirty miles away across the shining blue sea the snow-capped Olympic Mountains in the United States rose clear cut against the sky.

"Your house has the same view," Uncle Fred told the Lansdownes, "and it's built on the same plan, but it is cream, not white, and its roof is shingled in red, a pleasant red. Of course it is wood: there are very few brick or stone houses, except in the centre of the city. Directly you have finished tea we'll drive you on, get your luggage into the house and leave you to explore your new home alone. There's food enough for a day or two."

"I think you'll like to be alone, won't you?" Aunt

Susan asked. "But you're on the telephone, so do call us up if you want anything, though I hope you'll find all you want."

The Lansdownes were delighted with their new home.

"It's like a dream-house, or a ₁airy tale," Rosemary exclaimed.

The children were wild with excitement. They rushed from one room to another and through the veranda which ran round three sides of the house. The french windows of Michael's and Rosemary's little bedrooms opened on to a part of the veranda.

"Look, Mum, our beds are on wheels, they're out on the veranda now. May we really sleep here? And can we have all the windows open like this?" Michael bounced on to his bed and lay there. "I can see the sea and the mountains. How *spiffling*!"

Then the children rushed round the garden. It was not as big as many of the gardens round about, but Mr. Lansdowne was glad of this. It was big enough for him to manage. A sprinkler was spraying the lawn, which would have been dry and brown but for being watered several hours every day.

"Dad, come and look." Rosemary rushed into the house where her mother and father had begun unpacking what would be needed for the night. "Come and look at the strawberries and raspberries. May we pick them?"

"Yes, get a basin each and pick enough for supper, the ripest, and not too many."

When supper was over and everything tidied away, Mr. Lansdowne called the children from the garden.

"We'll have a little talk and a hymn and then we'll all go off to bed."

"Oh, must we! It's only eight o'clock!" Michael protested.

"Mother and I are very tired, and you must be too. Besides—you'll be sleeping on a veranda! Remember?"

Mr. Lansdowne asked God's blessing on their new home, and prayed that they might each one be helped to make it a happy, welcoming place to everyone who came.

"Now take a last run round the garden, and then bed," Mrs. Lansdowne said. "Yes, you can be out ten minutes or so."

Michael rushed out without waiting for Rosemary, and went down to the gate to look at the sea. He loved the sea, and it was wonderful to be living close to it. He stood watching purple shadows coming and going on the water turned rose-coloured by reflections from the sunset sky. The snow on the Olympic Mountains thirty miles away across the sea was a delicate rose colour too. The snow still lay more than half-way down the slopes. Would Dad take them to those mountains some day, he wondered. He would ask him.

Michael was startled by a boy about his own age calling across the road to him. The boy ran over when Michael said "Hullo!"

"Are you the new boy? Jolly good to have another boy living near. I'm Alf Stubbs. I live two doors down. They call me Stubby. Come across and I'll show you our little beach. There's a tiny one here, just under the headland. It's got a cave. It belongs to our club—five of us there are, but we could be six and let you join, if you're a real sport." Stubby looked Michael up and down. "We're the Vancouver Valiants."

Stubby pushed open the gate and Michael came out without thinking, and they ran across the road and down to a little sandy bay only a minute away. The Lansdownes' house was at the western end of the long sweep of Shoal Bay. The tiny beach to which Stubby took Michael was separated from the main bay by a reef of rocks, and sheltered on the other side by Gonzalees Head, a rocky headland rising to five hundred feet at its highest point. The road in front of the Lansdownes' house wound up and across it for three-quarters of a mile or so, and then descended to another wide sandy bay.

"There's a cave here." Stubby led Michael across the sands to the cliffs. "You have to crawl on your knees to get in. You'll be able to stand up inside. Come along. It's all right."

Michael didn't like the look of the entrance to the cave, and he knew he ought to run home at once. He ought not really to have come out of the garden.

Stubby saw Michael hesitating. "Come along, be a sport. It belongs to us Valiants. It's a good thing it's hard to get into. It makes it private."

Stubby lit a candle and Michael squeezed in. It was marvellous inside. "You are a sport," Stubby said warmly. "You see it's all right when you're in."

Michael glowed with Stubby's praise. If he'd refused to come in and gone home instead, he would have despised him. That would have been awful. Michael would just look round and then rush home.

The cave ran back ten feet or so and round it were rocky ledges.

"That's our larder along there." Stubby showed Michael a ledge four feet from the ground. "Not much grub in it now, but sometimes there's lots of stuff. That's my seaweed." He pointed to a layer of it in one corner. "It makes a jolly comfy bed, but our dads won't

let us sleep here at nights, worse luck. Come along, I'll
show you the way we Valiants get up to the headland.
We come down by the cliff way when we can. It keeps
the cave private."

Stubby pulled Michael along by the arm. "I must go
home," Michael stammered. "I must. Mum said be in
in ten minutes."

"Oh, what a baby you are! Going to bed, I suppose.
It won't hurt you to stay out a few minutes longer:
you're not sugar; you won't melt or anything, and
you've not been away ten minutes yet, anyway."

Michael nearly turned and ran, but he didn't dare.
Stubby would call him a baby if he ran home now, and
he'd never have any more to do with him, and he'd
never be asked to join the Valiants Club.

Stubby was already half-way up the cliff. The steps,
as he called them, started just outside the cave. Michael
began to scramble up. The quicker he was up the quicker
he'd get home. They were not steps, only cracks in the
cliff which the boys who knew them well used as foot-
holes. Stubby, showing off, took the climb at more of a
run than usual, while Michael slithered and slipped,
scratching and bruising his knees and breaking his
finger nails.

"I'll come down and help you," Stubby said grandly.
"You're only English, poor chap. You'll get into it *if*
you're the sporting sort, and then we might let you be a
Valiant. But you're awfully slow."

Michael was determined to be the right sort of chap,
so he struggled on with Stubby pulling him, and reached
the top on his knees and there he crouched, getting his
breath. He didn't dare even look at his cuts and bruises,
for fear Stubby should say he was soft and no sport at
all.

"You'll have to practise if you want to belong to the Valiants." Stubby spoke haughtily, and looked down scornfully at Michael, who still sat crouched on the ground.

"It would take me ages to get you down by the cliffs, and I must hurry home, you've been so awfully slow. *I'll* go by the cliffs, but it will be quicker for you to go by the road. You'll find it easily, just across there."

Michael couldn't humble himself to say, "Won't you come with me and show me the way," and before he had made up his mind how to ask Stubby to point out the track to the road, Stubby said, "I must skedaddle," and was gone. He seemed to drop straight over the edge and disappear. He certainly did climb well.

Michael rubbed his bruised knee and tied his handkerchief round the other, which had a jagged cut across the cap. Then he stood up and looked round. Where was the road? He could see nothing but rocks and sea. It must be on the side away from the sea, but there seemed no break in the rocks which ran up to a peak. There was really; the road was only twenty yards away, entirely hidden in a deep cutting; but Michael started clambering along parallel to it.

The sun had just set and cold air from the snow mountains caused a thick mist to form and shroud Gonzalees Head. Suddenly Michael was completely closed in by clouds. He could see nothing. He missed his footing and slipped and rolled six feet down with a crash that shook the breath out of him. When he struggled to his feet again, he had no idea which way to turn. The sound of the waves seemed to be all round him. At last he found a dry corner, and fell asleep.

Chapter Five

STUBBY'S REVENGE

R OSEMARY was the only one of the Lansdownes
who went to bed on that first night in Victoria.
She had no doubt that Michael would soon be
home again and fell asleep untroubled. Mr. Lansdowne
started to look for Michael as soon as he found out that
he was not in the garden, but after a short time the fog
came down and he knew that he would have to get help
in to search, as he did not know the district. He returned
home and telephoned to Fred Johnson.

They set out together, but could not do much except
go both ways along the road and shout. Michael did not
hear them: the rocks between them and the sound of the
waves splashing dulled their calls. His mother stayed in
the house alone. Mrs. Johnson had offered to come and
be with her, but Mrs. Lansdowne thought it would be
easier to be by herself. She did not want to discuss
Michael, or have more made of his wrong-doing than
need be. He had done wrong, of course; his mother
couldn't understand his going away without telling
them, after such a serious warning less than a week
before.

Mr. Lansdowne and Uncle Fred returned to the house
every hour or so to see if Michael had by any chance
found his way back. It was Uncle Fred who found him
as the fog lifted with the first light of dawn. Michael
had slept on and off in spite of the chilly mist around
him. Silver bars were shimmering across the delicate

blue of the sea as Uncle Fred helped him up the rocks and along the road home.

No morning could outwardly have dawned more splendidly for the Lansdownes' first day in Victoria, but the very beauty of the day made the family feel more unhappy. By the time Rosemary was awake Michael was in bed. There was nothing seriously wrong with him, though his bruised and cut knees were stiff and aching. His mother darkened the room and hoped that he would soon fall asleep. She was very grieved at the defiance and temper he had shown.

Michael was really troubled, and knew that he had done wrong. He realized that he had upset his mother and father badly, but when he had got home he had pretended that he was not to blame at all, and that it was very unfair to treat him as if he had done something awful. Perhaps he would have said he was sorry at once, but as Uncle Fred was bringing him home he had demanded an explanation, and then spoken very severely, more severely than Michael had ever been spoken to.

"It's disgraceful to have behaved like this," he had said. "You knew quite well you were doing wrong, so stop pretending. You were just showing off to Stubby, and not thinking at all of your parents."

"I was thinking of them. I tell you I was," Michael blurted out. "I couldn't possibly help what happened. Stubby made me go up the cliffs. I didn't want to."

"Well, then you're a weak sort of a chap as well as being untrustworthy and unkind. If you were my boy I should punish you severely, but Geoff would never behave like this."

Michael arrived home furiously angry. Uncle Fred had not meant to make matters worse. He was kind-hearted and fond of boys, but he wanted Michael to realize how seriously he had distressed his parents.

His parents sat with him while he ate some breakfast. They expected Michael would say how sorry he was, but instead he repeated. "I couldn't help it, Dad. I tell you I couldn't help it. It wasn't my fault. I meant to be back in ten minutes. You didn't tell me not to leave the garden. It isn't fair, Uncle Fred going for me. It isn't my fault there was a sea-fog. The fog might have happened to anyone."

"You had better go to bed and to sleep, Michael," his father said. "We don't want to talk to you while you're in a temper."

But Michael could not go to sleep. He only wished that he could. He lay tossing in bed, knowing that he had only added to the trouble, by being defiant. "If only I had said at once that I knew I ought not to have left the garden and gone to the shore with Stubby and to the cave and up the cliffs! I did it just because I wanted Stubby to like me and think I was a sport. I've not been valiant, or God's pilgrim. I've been scared of what Stubby would say."

Michael tossed about for a while longer going through and through things. "If only Uncle Fred hadn't gone for me and I hadn't got in such a rage!"

Then Michael lay still for a few minutes and found that he was praying to God to help him. God understood all about it, why he was so miserable, and why he had been defiant and horrid to his mum and dad. He knew as he prayed what was the right thing to do, and that God would give him courage to do it.

"I'm a bit like the Prodigal Son," he thought. "I will arise and go to my father, and say I've done wrong. Oh God, help me, please help me."

Before there was time to finish his prayer, he sprang out of bed and went to the door and called, "Mum, Dad."

They were both in the house and came to his room. "I want to say something," he said, "I want to very badly. I was wrong to go out of the garden and go with Stubby. I wanted Stubby to think I was brave and sporting, but I wasn't. I know now. I've been praying. I feel inside that God has forgiven me. Please do forgive me." Michael looked up at his parents, imploring. "I really and truly mean never to do anything like it again, because I know I've made you unhappy."

His mother stooped and gave him a hug and a kiss. "Of course we forgive you, Michael," and they both smiled at him. "Now, dear, you have a sleep. I'll call you in time to be ready for dinner."

And Michael, knowing that he was forgiven by God and his parents, fell asleep in a few minutes, so that the family were happier at the midday meal than it seemed possible that they could have been a few hours before.

At dinner Mr. Lansdowne told the children that they were starting school the very next morning. They were not going to the same school as Anne and Geoff because that school was full up, but to the International School in town.

"Whatever is an International School?" Rosemary asked.

"It's a famous school in Victoria where there are boys and girls of a number of different nationalities. All the teaching is in English," Mr. Lansdowne added quickly, when Rosemary looked scared. "Just now there are Danes, Norwegians, Germans, Swiss, Japanese and Chinese, and there may be boys and girls from other countries. Of course there are more Canadians than any other nationality."

Michael checked himself from saying that he didn't want to go to a school where there were girls. He must try to fit in with what was planned.

"I'm a bit scared," Rosemary exclaimed, "though it's thrilling in a way, and I'm glad we're starting school."

"You needn't be scared, dear," her mother said. "I'm sure everyone will be kind and welcoming."

At half-past eight the next morning, Uncle Fred drove round for Michael and Rosemary. Mr. and Mrs. Lansdowne went too. Mr. Lansdowne was dropped close to his office and Mrs. Lansdowne went on to the school with the children. She was to have a talk with the headmaster.

When the headmaster had welcomed Michael and Rosemary, a boy called Dan Summers, a few months older than Michael, took him to his form-master and then showed him the swimming baths and playing fields, and told him what jolly good times they had, and Michael began to be glad they were pupils at the International School.

There were more boys than girls in his form and that pleased him, and he found that he was a form higher than Rosemary. This was a relief: lessons came easier to her than to him and he had to work hard to keep ahead of her. There were thirty in Michael's form, and it was not till the boys were leaving the room for the ten minutes break before dinner that Michael came on Stubby. His desk was at the back of the room.

"Hullo, tell-tale!" Stubby took care to speak so that all the boys near could hear. "You're a sneak, you are. So it's my fault you're a sissy?"

The blood rushed to Michael's face till he was scarlet with anger. It all happened so suddenly.

"I'm not a tell-tale. I'm not a sissy. How dare you call me one!"

Stubby was enjoying Michael's anger, and the gaping crowd of boys that clustered round them.

"You're the meanest sneak I've ever seen. Who said I forced you to come to the shore and the cave and forced you to climb up onto the headland? I didn't force you. I was just being decent to a new chap. You *are* a sissy." Stubby looked round at the circle of boys and spoke to them. "What do you think the goon did, he lay down in a gully and blubbed, and stayed there till Mr. Johnson found him and carried the great baby home, and Dad whacked *me* for it! I tell you *he* ought to have been whacked, not me."

More boys joined the crowd. They loved a row. It looked as if there might even be a fight.

"It's all lies !" Michael blurted out. "I didn't blub."

"You call me a liar !" Stubby shouted, and advanced on Michael, who prepared to defend himself.

Dan Summers was just in time to pull Michael away.

"Come along, Mr. Maudsley wants you," he shouted above the hubbub, and he dragged Michael forcibly away.

Mr. Maudsley did want Michael, though only to arrange where Michael was to sit at dinner.

"You'd jolly well better keep out of Stubby's way for a bit," Dan told Michael afterwards. "He's a decent chap, really, but you got him into a row with his dad. Of course he oughtn't to have left you, but he is mad that he was whacked. Were you whacked?"

"No, Dad doesn't believe in whacking boys."

"Hum!" ejaculated Dan. "I hope Stubby thinks you

were. You had better keep out of his way at school and at home too. It'll blow over, but it may take a bit of time."

"But I didn't blub, and he did make me climb up, and he did leave me without showing me the road, and he knew I couldn't have got home before the fog came."

"Look here, kid, if you want to get on at school show some real pluck now, and just you shut up and don't tell the tale to anyone else. That'll be a really decent thing to do. And keep out of Stubby's way. I'll stick up for you, if you say no more about it."

So Michael shut his mouth tight and said no more.

The three weeks before the end of the term slipped quickly by. Rosemary had been very happy and had never once wished that she were back in Southampton. If only Stubby were not at the International School, Michael would have been happy too; but Stubby seized every chance of jeering at Michael and teasing him. Michael avoided quarrelling, and gradually other boys as well as Dan Summers stuck up for him.

"It'll be all right next term," Dan assured Michael, "you may be pals, some time."

On the first day of the holidays, Michael and Rosemary started to build a raft. There were three Flynn children, a girl Michael's age and two boys about Rosemary's age; they came to the beach every day, and they helped Michael and Rosemary to start. A good deal of wood was washed up on the beach of Shoal Bay, for waste pieces from a nearby sawmill were left on the shore near the mill and washed out to the sea and then carried by winds and currents into the bays round about.

Julie Flynn had given them a wooden box, into which

two children could just squeeze, but they needed more wood than they could find on the beach of Shoal Bay, for they must make a float on which to place the box so that it would not sink.

"Ask your mum and dad to let us take you to Oak Bay to get more wood," said Julie. "There's always wood there. The currents wash it up. The bay is less than a mile away, but it will have to be tomorrow. It's teatime now, and Mummy's taking us to the Crystal Baths this evening."

"Where are they?" Michael asked eagerly.

"They're close to the Grand Hotel near the harbour. It's lovely swimming and diving there, because it's deep, and not shallow and cold like it is here."

"Oh, I do wish we could come with you!" Rosemary said longingly.

"Well, I'm sure Mummy would love to take you," Julie said. "I'm sure she would. We don't mind squashes in the car a bit. You ring us up, will you, and we'll call for you if it's all right for you to come? It will be great fun having you."

Michael and Rosemary ran home to tea very excited. They were thrilled at the thought of getting wood from Oak Bay, and of going to the Crystal Baths with the Flynns. They ran their fastest, for they were in a hurry to ask their parents, but when they reached the road they saw Uncle Fred's car in front of their gate. Uncle Fred and Aunt Susan! Why ever had they come? They might advise their parents not to let them go to the Crystal Baths nor to Oak Bay with the Flynns. They had an unhappy feeling that things were not going to turn out well, and unluckily they turned out even worse than Michael and Rosemary expected.

Chapter Six

ROSEMARY RUNS AWAY

THE Johnson family were all in the veranda talking and laughing, but they rose to go as Rosemary and Michael entered.

"No, we're not staying to tea," Aunt Susan said, as she smiled at Michael and Rosemary. "We've just been settling a lovely surprise for you two. Yes, a lovely one," she added as the children looked gloomy about it.

"Please, what?" asked Rosemary, who suddenly had a feeling that Aunt Susan's surprise would prevent them from going to Oak Bay, and perhaps to the baths too. Since Michael's night on Gonzalees Head, Anne and Geoff had been a bit severe with their young cousins. Rosemary enjoyed playing with the Flynns far more than going to the Johnsons, for she was shy and frightened there.

"Your dad and mum will tell you all about it," Aunt Susan said in a rather mysterious voice.

Michael as well as Rosemary was sure the surprise couldn't be half as jolly as going to this Crystal Baths and Oak Bay with the Flynns.

Mr. Lansdowne walked down the garden with the visitors to the car and saw them off and then came back smiling.

"Please tell us quick what the surprise is, Mum," Rosemary asked her mother anxiously. And then not waiting for her mother to reply, she said, "Please may we ask you two things first? May we go to the Crystal Baths with the Flynns this evening? Mrs. Flynn will drive us, and may we go with them to Oak Bay tomorrow?"

Mr. Lansdowne had returned in time to hear what Rosemary asked. The children read hesitation on their parents' faces. "Please do let us," Michael begged. "We want wood to finish our raft, and they say it's spiffling at the Crystal Baths; and they want us to go, really they do."

"Sit down to tea now, dears," Mrs. Lansdowne said, "and we will talk about it."

Looking very troubled the children sat down. "Now we're ready. Do, do please say yes," Rosemary begged.

It was Mr. Lansdowne who answered.

"I'm afraid you can't go to Oak Bay tomorrow. You'll have to go some other day. You see, Uncle Fred and Aunt Susan have invited you to go up the island with them tomorrow to camp at Qualicum Bay. Well, it isn't exactly camping, for they have a chalet there close to the sands. They can sleep six, three rooms with two berths in each. It's very kind of them to ask you. You're starting directly after breakfast tomorrow. You'll have a splendid time," Mr. Lansdowne added, for he quickly saw that the children did not want to go.

"Oh, Mum, don't, please don't make us go." Rosemary went over to her mother and leaned against her pleadingly. "I'll hate it without you. They don't really want us. They're just thinking they're being nice."

"I don't want to go!" Michael announced. "Geoff doesn't like me. He scorns me and bosses me. They've invited us to teach us to behave. We do try, and it's horrid being put right all the time. Oh, Mum, why did you say we'd go without asking us?"

"But, children, we're quite sure you'll enjoy it when you get there. It's a splendid bathing place. It doesn't get cold currents from glaciers like Shoal Bay, and there will be ponies, and Uncle Fred says he will teach you to ride. You've always wanted to learn to ride, haven't you?"

"But, Mummy, I can't bear to go without you. I want to stay with you. I don't want to learn to ride. Do say I needn't go," Rosemary tried to be brave, and she blinked back tears.

"We can't change what is arranged now; it would not be polite or kind." Rosemary went back to her place and tried to finish her tea, but it was hard work.

"I don't want to go either," Michael declared. "I like it at home. I know Uncle Fred wants to get me away from Stubby, that's partly why he's asked us, but I shall keep out of Stubby's way all right here."

Mr. and Mrs. Lansdowne were distressed that the children were so upset about going, and they were uneasy because Michael had guessed one of the reasons for the invitation, that he should be away from Stubby. But they consoled themselves by the certainty that Uncle Fred and Aunt Susan would undoubtedly give them a good time.

Seeing that Michael and Rosemary were so troubled about the visit to Qualicum Bay Mrs. Lansdowne decided to let them go to the Crystal Baths, if Mrs. Flynn really had room for them and wanted them. She went off to the telephone and came back smiling.

"Now, cheer up, my ducks," she said. "Get your coats and run along to the Flynns'. You are asked to go and swim and dive, and then stay and have supper in the restaurant afterwards and watch a special diving show. It'll be a lovely treat for you. I didn't mean you to

have a late night, but we'll get you awake and dressed
in time in the morning."

For a week Rosemary tried her hardest to make the
best of things. Qualicum was a beautiful place, the most
beautiful place to which she had ever been. The sea
was warm on the sandy shore, and Aunt Susan let the
children stay in as long as they liked.

At first, no one was exactly unkind to Rosemary,
though Anne made her feel unwanted and kept putting
her right about little things. Rosemary would have put
up with that if she had not felt so terribly, hopelessly
homesick. She was miserable all over with homesickness.
She had never been away from her mother for one single
night before, and she felt very much alone and unloved.
Each night she cried herself to sleep, waking with a
headache and feeling as if something even more awful
was going to happen to her. No one knew that she cried
at night. She didn't mean to cry, but she just couldn't
help it. Anne did not come to the berth in the room
which they were sharing till Rosemary was worn out
with tears and either asleep or pretending to be asleep.

Everything was so strange. She grew more and more
shy. She did not know what room she ought to be in or
what she ought to do when nothing special was happen-
ing. Anne said sharp little things that hurt and frightened her. She became afraid of everyone except Michael,
and hardly looked up from her plate at meals. Uncle
Fred tried to draw her into things by teasing her in a
kindly way, but she couldn't laugh, she was afraid she
would cry and not be able to stop, and that would be
awful.

Rosemary might have endured another week if Anne
had not scolded her for being glum and not showing

gratitude to Uncle Fred and Aunt Susan for having her at Qualicum. That was more than Rosemary could bear. She hung her head and did not speak, trying not to cry.

"Can't you say you're sorry?" Anne said, vexed at Rosemary's silence.

Rosemary rushed away, and Anne, thinking that at last she had made an impression on her sulky little cousin, went off to bathe, supposing Rosemary would follow when she had recovered from her ill temper, but Rosemary escaped out of the back door of the chalet without anyone seeing her and fled into the wood behind the house. She threw herself into the long grass under the trees and sobbed.

Anne noticed that Rosemary did not come down to bathe, but she was not worried—she hoped she had taught her a lesson. Anne did not notice that Michael did not stay in the water long. She and Geoff swam out to the raft anchored in the bay and forgot their cousins. They had not wanted them invited to Qualicum—they had wanted two friends of their own to join the party. Uncle Fred and Aunt Susan had gone off for the day to Cameron Lake to search for orchids in the forests that bordered it.

As soon as Michael missed Rosemary, he dressed quickly and slipped away from the shore. He knew that she was desperately homesick and he was upset about it. Anne was being unkind, he was sure, and Rosemary minded things so. No one understood how she minded. He had meant to pluck up courage to ask Uncle Fred to take her home. He kept repeating to himself what he meant to say. "Please will you take Rosemary home? She's so miserable away from Mummy. I'll stay if you want me to." But just when he hoped to get a chance of speaking to Uncle Fred alone he found he was going away for the day, and he was not alone one minute before he and Aunt Susan set out together.

It was half an hour before Michael found Rosemary. She had come to an end of her tears, and was sitting up dismally.

"I'm going to run away now and get home by this evening," she told Michael. "Don't tell me not to, please. I can't bear another day here, and nights are awful, and Anne has just gone for me. She . . ." but Rosemary's lips quivered and tears came into her eyes again.

"Oh, please don't!" Michael begged. "I'm going to ask Uncle Fred to take you home. I'll ask him directly he gets back. I promise I will."

"But he won't take me. I know he won't. Anne says I've got to learn to be sensible and grateful, but I can't. Do go and fetch my purse and I'll go."

"But I shan't let you go alone, I couldn't. We'll start now. Perhaps I can get back here by this evening."

If Michael and Rosemary had stopped to think they would have known that they would cause great anxiety both to the Johnsons and their parents by running away from Qualicum without telling anyone, but Rosemary was ill with misery and Michael felt that he must protect and help her.

There was another thought in his mind, too. Ever since they had reached Victoria they had lived in a whirl of excitement—there were so many new and thrilling things to do. But they had been puzzled and even worried by the difficulties of settling down among new people. The Canadian boys and girls seemed to look down on them and treat them as if they were babies. They thought that they had to ask leave to do quite ordinary things, and never acted independently. Well, they were acting independently now. That is how running away seemed to Michael. To Rosemary it was the only thing to do. She must get away from Anne and back to her mother.

Michael tiptoed into the chalet to get their purses. Anne and Geoff were still bathing. They had nearly ten dollars between them. They would be able to pay for tickets by train or bus for most of the way. Michael thought it was not more than eighty miles.

For the first mile they were terrified of meeting one of the Johnsons' many friends, but when they had passed the last houses of Qualicum village they felt less strained. The road had been quiet. They thought that no one had noticed them, and no cars had passed.

"Let's go into the woods here and you can have a rest for a few minutes. You look all in. We shall be hidden," said Michael, leading the way. "We must make plans."

But they found that they could not really plan anything, because they did not know how far it was to the nearest place where the buses stopped. There was a railway, but Michael was afraid that they might be questioned and stopped if they bought tickets at a station.

"Someone will offer us a lift some time, I'm sure," Michael said stoutly. He was certain they would; but then a fear came to him that he did not tell Rosemary. Anyone who picked them up would ask questions. They would want to know where they had come from and where they were going. They might even insist on taking them back to the Johnsons.

"Oh, dear," Michael thought to himself, "I believe I ought to take Rosemary back to Qualicum. We're not far away yet."

Michael looked at his sister. She was nearly asleep, and looked white and ill. While he was thinking how to begin persuading her to go back, she smiled and said, "Oh, it is lovely to be away from them. Do you think it would be safe for me to go properly to sleep for just a little while?"

"I don't know," Michael spoke hesitatingly. "Suppose we go on a little further—unless you'd like to go back?"

Rosemary sat up in horror. "You don't understand, Michael. You don't know how horrid Anne's been. You can go if you want to, but I won't go back *ever*."

Rosemary began to cry and lay down again in despair. She thought Michael would have understood. In a few minutes her sobs ceased and Michael saw that she was asleep. It was no use for him to blame Anne or Geoff. If it had not been for him they would never have been asked to Qualicum, and Michael had an uncomfortable feeling that he was the cause of it all. If only he hadn't gone off with Stubby on the first evening and got lost in the fog! He was awfully unlucky—and then having Stubby at the same school and living so near . . . He'd never be asked to be a Vancouver Valiant now. He'd always have to potter about with the Flynns.

Well, he could be valiant in a way, he'd get Rosemary home to Mum. He looked with pity at Rosemary's tear-stained face. He ought to have done something to help her before. It had been awful for her, being so unhappy.

After what seemed a long time to Michael, Rosemary opened her eyes, rubbed them and sat up. "I feel better," she said. "Let's go on, and get further away from them."

They began to tramp along the Island Highway. It was hard going, and sandals were poor footgear for a long walk. Their feet soon became sore and tired. A few cars overtook them, but no driver offered the children a lift, and Michael dared not ask for one so near Qualicum.

Chapter Seven

MR. CHISHOLM TO THE RESCUE

"I CAN'T go any further, Michael," Rosemary moaned, sinking down on the grass at the roadside. "Do try to make a car stop, Michael, please do."

Michael gazed up the road. No cars were coming. Then a motor-bus appeared, labelled Victoria. It was travelling fast. Michael signalled furiously, but it seemed to increase its speed, rather than slow down. It was an express-bus, only stopping at villages and towns.

"Come on, just a little farther," Michael urged. "Perhaps we're coming to a village."

After about half a mile, they reached the outskirts of a town. "There must be buses from here," Michael said.

They trudged on. Rosemary had a bad blister on her heel, but in spite of this she limped along bravely. In a square in the centre of the town a number of buses were waiting.

"You sit on that seat," Michael told Rosemary. "I'll go and look where they're going."

But there was not a bus to Victoria, though there was one to Duncan. Michael was sure Duncan was on the way to Victoria. Trying to be brave and appear unanxious he went up to the driver and conductor who were standing by the bus talking, and asked them if they were starting soon.

"Yes, we're off in a few minutes, at half-past twelve. We get to Duncan a bit before four."

"Is it a slow bus then?" Michael asked. It seemed to him to take a very long time.

"We go round a bit by villages, but there's nothing will get you there sooner. You've missed the express bus."

The conductor did not take any special interest in the children and when Michael had booked their tickets, which only cost three dollars, as they were both half-fares, they settled down with relief. But they did not go unnoticed. A lady travelling on the bus thought Rosemary looked ill, and that it was strange that two children should be going as far as Duncan alone, and with no sandwiches. She ate her lunch as soon as the bus started and then gave some sandwiches and buns to the children. Michael ate heartily, but she noticed that Rosemary took only one bite of a sandwich and then leant against Michael and closed her eyes.

"Is your sister not feeling well?" the lady asked Michael a little before the bus reached the village where she was getting off.

"She's feeling a bit ill," Michael replied, "but I'm taking her home. She'll be all right when she gets to Mummy."

"Is someone meeting you in Duncan?"

"No," Michael admitted reluctantly. "But we'll be all right, thank you," he added.

"Are you sure I can't help you?" she asked.

But before Michael could reply the bus stopped, and the conductor hurried her off, for the bus was already late.

Michael studied the bus timetable posted inside the bus. He was delighted to see that there was a bus leaving Duncan for Victoria at four. The conductor had said they would reach Duncan a bit before four, so they would be able to catch the four o'clock all right. Then they would be home by half-past six. Michael could hardly believe this. It seemed too wonderful to be true.

Rosemary was fast asleep. Michael wished he knew how the time was going, but he had no watch and he did not like to ask the conductor. When the road began to pass between houses he thought that they might be nearing Duncan, and he woke Rosemary. "We've got to catch the four o'clock bus from Duncan," he told her, "and I think this is the beginning of it."

The bus turned off the highway into the town square. Michael caught sight of a clock: it was ten minutes past four. Of course the bus to Victoria had gone. He didn't even ask anyone. He tried not to show his misery and disappointment to Rosemary.

"We must just walk the little bit back to the highway, then we're sure to get a lift. It'll be quicker than the bus," he added cheerfully. "I'll signal everyone to stop. Look, here's a fruit-shop. Let's buy some peaches to cheer us up."

They reached the highway and Michael began to eat a peach while they waited, but Rosemary would not begin hers at once.

"I must tell you something, Michael," she said. "I know now I oughtn't to have run away. It seemed all right when we started, but now I'm sure I ought not to have done it, and I made you do it, too."

Michael was so taken aback that he did not say anything. It was easier to think you oughtn't to have run away when you had got away from the people you were frightened of. Well, they couldn't possibly go back now.

Rosemary seemed less miserable after telling Michael this and began to eat her peach, but suddenly a wasp settled on it. She hit at it with her other hand, and it flew into her face and stung her just under her eye. She dropped her peach and jumped up, crying with pain. All round her eye swelled up quickly till she could not see. She bent double with pain and moaned. Michael made her sit down. "Keep your hand over it," he said, and as wasps were buzzing round them he threw all the peaches as far away as he could into the bushes, hoping the wasps would follow them.

"Oh God! please send a car quick and a kind person," Michael prayed as he had never prayed before. "Please make the next car pick us up and take us home. Please forgive us. It didn't seem so wrong when we started! I don't know what to do about Rosemary."

At that moment a bus turned into the highway coming from Duncan. It was the Victoria bus, twenty minutes or so late. Then two cars passed. They were full. Then all was silent in the brooding heat of late afternoon, only poor Rosemary's sobs broke the stillness.

At last Michael heard a car coming. He must stop this car. He would stand right in the way. The driver must see they needed help. He stretched out both arms and waved, but there was no need to do anything really, for the driver had seen the children from a distance and had been watching Rosemary. She was clearly in distress. The driver drew up to the side of the road and jumped out. "Why!" he exclaimed amazed. "It's Michael and Rosemary!" He was Mr. Chisholm, the minister of the church which they were attending in Victoria.

"Whatever are you two doing here!" Then he turned to Rosemary. "Child, what has happened?" he asked gently, putting his arm round her shoulders. Sympathy brought fresh tears, but oh, Rosemary was so thankful to see Mr. Chisholm, and perhaps Michael was more thankful still. Mr. Chisholm helped her into the car.

"Come and sit in front too," he told Michael. "There's room for three of us. We're near a village and I'll take Rosemary to the doctor there and get something done to her eye."

Mr. Chisholm asked no questions then, for it was clear that Michael was almost as distressed as his sister. Dr. Taylor was a friend of Mr. Chisholm's and saw Rosemary at once.

"It's a bad sting, and a nasty place to be stung. You're a brave girl," he said. Rosemary gave him a watery smile. "But you're limping. What's up with your foot? Let's have a look at it. A bad blister, that is. There now, that'll be more comfortable."

Dr. Taylor turned to Mr. Chisholm: "See, I'll give her two tablets. She's had a nasty shock. Let her lie down in the back of the car. She'll sleep." And Dr. Taylor and Mr. Chisholm settled Rosemary in the car with a rug tucked round her.

"Now, Michael, tell me what's up," Mr. Chisholm said. "I must telephone your parents. Dr. Taylor will let me use his phone, but what am I to say to them?"

Michael told him all about their dreadful day, and he got on to the Lansdownes and the Johnsons. He knew the Johnsons well, and though Michael had told him very little about Qualicum, he understood how homesick a child like Rosemary might be with Anne and Geoff, and even with Mrs. Johnson.

Michael sat silently in the front of the car until Mr. Chisholm joined him. Though he did not speak Mr. Chisholm knew how troubled he was.

"Tell me how it all began, Michael, if you would like

to. It would be better than going over and over it inside, wouldn't it?"

"Yes, it would." Michael sighed with relief. "I really didn't mean to do wrong," he began. "I wish I'd told Uncle Fred how home-sick Rosemary was! You see, she was quite ill with it."

"It must have been very hard for you, and it is no good now wishing you had done something different. We all make mistakes. The great thing is to own we have been wrong and to ask God to forgive us and anyone we have hurt."

"I have asked God to forgive me. I shall ask Dad and Mum directly we get home to forgive me, but I don't know what to do about Uncle Fred. I suppose we hurt him, and Aunt Susan, and perhaps Anne, but I don't want to ask Anne to forgive me. She was so horrid to Rosemary!"

There was silence for a few minutes. Then Mr. Chisholm said, "You know what Jesus taught us to pray about forgiving and being forgiven, don't you?"

"Yes, forgive us as we forgive other people."

"It seems as if you will have to try to forgive Anne before you feel quite happy, and perhaps Aunt Susan and Uncle Fred for not seeing that Rosemary was miserable. I don't mean that you should talk to them about it, but forgive them in your heart and thoughts."

"It would be jolly hard to forgive Anne," Michael said, "I don't know if I can."

"There is only one way. Ask God to help you and to help you to see why Anne acted as she did, and to see the nice things in her. When you've done that, you needn't think about her any more."

"But I've got to say I'm sorry to Uncle Fred and ask him to forgive me. I wish I hadn't got to. You see,

Uncle Fred thinks I'm awful, and I am sort of to blame for all this. We should never have had to go and stay with them at Qualicum but for me. Uncle Fred wanted to keep me out of Stubby's way."

Michael went on to explain about going off with him the first evening and being out all night on Gonzalees Head and about being at the same school. Mr. Chisholm had heard already more of this than Michael knew.

"Well, that's all over and done with now," Mr. Chisholm told Michael. "What you have to do is to think of the best way of showing Uncle Fred and Aunt Susan that you are really sorry for the anxiety you have caused them. There's always a right thing to do at any moment and God will help you to see what it is."

Michael felt so much happier after talking to Mr. Chisholm that he lay back in the car and went to sleep. When the car drew up in front of their home both children were sleeping. Michael woke with a start when he heard his father speaking to Mr. Chisholm.

"We are so grateful to you," his father was saying. "What a mercy you came upon them."

Michael was wide awake again. "I prayed hard for someone kind to come, and God sent Mr. Chisholm. That's how it happened," he told his father. Then he turned and saw his mother hurrying to the gate. He ran to her and she took him in her arms and hugged him, and he knew that, whatever he had to do about telling Uncle Fred that he was sorry, nothing mattered, for his father and mother understood and loved him and he was home again.

Chapter Eight

BACK TO QUALICUM

MICHAEL woke early after sleeping right through the night from eight o'clock in the evening. He dressed quickly and went as far as the gate and stood watching the sun. It had just risen above the eastern mountains, flooding the sea with gold. The children at the Sunday School in Victoria to which Michael and Rosemary went said a prayer together each Sunday thanking God for all the lovely things of which they could think. So here it was natural for Michael to thank God for the clear sky and the sparkling sea and the exciting feeling of being alive, and being at home with his father and mother.

Then he remembered that in some way he had to tell Uncle Fred and Aunt Susan how sorry he was that he had made them anxious, and he remembered too that Mr. Chisholm had told him that there was always a right thing to do whatever muddles you had made; and as he watched the changing colours in the sea it came to him quite clearly that God wanted him to go back to Qualicum, to Uncle Fred and Aunt Susan, that very day, and stay the week and be as decent as he could.

"I don't want to, but I'll have to do it," he told himself. "I'll have to, if they'll have me."

Michael hurried back to the house. His mother was in the kitchen.

"Mummy," he began, "I think I ought to go back to Qualicum today. May I, if I pay the fare from my pocket-money? I'll be as decent as I can. I won't let them mind having me. You know in the Pilgrim Hymn —about disaster, and following the Master. I want to try."

"I am glad, Michael. I'm sure Dad will be glad, too, and proud of you. We'll get him to telephone."

At midday Michael was standing at the railway-carriage window feeling all quivery inside—like he did before running the hundred yards. The train was passing the first houses of Qualicum. The train drew into the station. The frightened feelings vanished, for there was Uncle Fred on the platform waving to him, and there was Geoff too. The three of them squashed into the front of the car. It was more friendly like that. Aunt Susan and Anne were waiting in the road outside the garden to welcome Michael. He just managed to say, "I'm awfully sorry," to Uncle Fred and Aunt Susan, but there was no chance to say more, because they all began to talk about a visit to Woodport planned for the afternoon.

Woodport is on an inlet of the Pacific, on the opposite side of Vancouver Island to Qualicum. It lies in a fold of the foothills surrounded by forests, so that the party did not see the huge factories and timber yards till they were close to them.

"Look!" exclaimed Geoff. "Look at the steamers loading up, and look at the people! It's like a big town."

"Well, it is a town now," Mr. Johnson told them. "It was a tiny village before the huge timber mills were built."

The party was first taken to a part of the mill where eight-foot-long pieces of thick tree trunks were being twisted round against a long and very sharp blade and made into flat boards. It looked just as if a huge roll of paper were being unrolled and laid out flat.

Seeing Michael's keenness, the man who was working the machinery called to him. "Come over here, young chap," he said, "and you shall unroll a log." He showed Michael which levers to raise and when to lower them, and Michael was amazed when he found that he had cut a great log into a flat piece eight feet by ten.

Michael would have liked to stay and work the slicer all afternoon, but Uncle Fred called him to come along. There was lots more to see. They watched the making of three-ply and of doors and window frames, planks, chairs and tables, all turned out by machinery.

After an hour and a half had passed very quickly, the manager came to speak to Mr. Johnson. "I'm so glad you have enjoyed what you've seen. Now wouldn't those boys of yours like some pieces of wood to take home, pieces for raft-building, perhaps?"

Geoff and Michael were filled with excitement. "May I have some too?" Anne asked.

The manager saw that they did not know what to choose from a shed full of odd pieces of wood which to them all looked very good, so he chose for them what would be suitable for raft-building, and the party started home with as much wood as could be packed into the boot of the car and piled up on their knees.

"I am so glad I came back," Michael was thinking as they drove back to Qualicum by the forest road from which they caught glimpses of deer and bears.

Geoff and Michael were rather disappointed when Mr. Johnson told them that they must not start building the rafts at Qualicum, because, though they had two cars, they could not possibly take finished rafts home to

Victoria with all the other luggage. There was only just enough room to take the wood.

But they soon got over their disappointment, for the weather was fine and warm and Geoff began to teach Michael life-saving.

"You're really a game chap," he told Michael, and Michael glowed with pride. "You'll be ready to enter for the preliminary life-saving tests by the end of August," and Michael was as set on being fit to enter as Geoff to train him. Nothing could have made the cousins firmer friends.

Rosemary rushed down the garden to meet Michael when she saw Uncle Fred's car come round the corner. She had been very lonely without him; they had never been apart for one day before. The Flynns had befriended her, taking her to the Crystal Baths and for picnics, but nothing made up for Michael being away.

Geoff, Michael, Rosemary, Anne, the Flynns and Mr. Chisholm's boy of fourteen, as well as many onlookers, came each morning and afternoon of the next week, either to make or watch the making of three rafts. Mr. Chisholm came twice. He and his son were skilled at building sea-worthy rafts. By the end of the week the rafts were painted and ready to launch.

When the raft trials were over and Mr. Flynn had declared all three craft seaworthy, a day was arranged for a picnic on Half-Moon Island, which lay a mile out beyond Gonzalees Head. Anne, Geoff, the Flynns and Lansdownes made up the party, and Mr. Flynn and Mr. Lansdowne each took out a motor-boat of picnickers, while the raft-makers went on their rafts, sailing when the wind helped them and paddling too.

It was a cloudless afternoon towards the end of

August when the fleet set sail. Half-Moon Island was a grand place for picnics. There was a bathing beach that shelved quickly, making the water deep, overhanging rocks from which bathers could dive, and good trees for climbing.

Tide and wind were favourable as the party sailed to the island. It was the kind of glowing afternoon that made everyone feel extra happy, and the rafters were delighted with the way their craft behaved. All the Lansdownes were thinking what a wonderful place Victoria was.

After tree-climbing, a long bathe and tea with a fire built on the beach, everyone lay in the sun comfortably lazy, except Mr. Flynn, who went in search of a special heather that he was keen to find. When he had climbed to the highest point of the island he was startled to see clouds filling up in wreathing masses over the mountains. Already the breeze had freshened. He knew at once that a gale was on its way. Easterly gales did not usually sweep over Victoria till September, but it was now the end of August. He hurried back and called Mr. Lansdowne aside, pretending to hand him the heather.

"That gale will break over us in half an hour and may last two days," he told Mr. Lansdowne. "The rafts must be left in the shelter of the bushes here, and all of us go back in the two boats. We'll try not to alarm the party, but we must go at once."

They were off in ten minutes. The boys and girls enjoyed the excitement at first, but the waves were rising quickly, whipped up by the wind. They rushed along and lifted the boats and then banged them down with a crash, making them pitch from end to end as well as rolling from side to side.

Everyone was alarmed, too alarmed to be sick. "Don't look at the waves. Get low in the boat," Mr. Flynn advised. The main force of the wind was behind them, so fortunately they were being driven towards the shore, but scores of logs which seemed to appear from no-where were being hurled about in the waves. They had at some time broken loose from log-rafts being towed from forests and saw-mills. Some were as big as full grown trees. It was hard to see when they were coming close, for besides the blinding rain, sheets of spray and waves hid the trunks.

The last half-mile was a grim struggle, with waves breaking right over and into the boats. A group of anxious people had gathered and were watching the two boats, sometimes entirely hidden from the shore. They could do nothing but plunge into the waves and help haul the boats ashore when they were near enough.

Mr. Flynn's boat was in first. It was caught up by a great wave and hurled ashore, grounding with a thud. A dozen pairs of hands were on it in a moment, hauling it and its passengers as far up the beach as they could. Quickly the children were pulled out and bundled up on to the road.

Mr. Lansdowne's boat was driven in ten yards farther down the shore. Rosemary was lifted out and carried home. The boys and girls were all thankful to be at home and in bed, and Mrs. Flynn and Mrs. Lansdowne did not go out again, but almost everyone who lived near Shoal Bay went on to the coast road and watched the great waves rushing towards the shore, carrying logs with them. The waves seemed to grow bigger and bigger every few minutes. An hour after the boats had managed to get in, spray from the waves was dashing over the road, and the waves were pounding the cliffs. In the turmoil of wind and water hundreds of logs were being thrown hither and thither as if they were no bigger than matches.

Many people stayed up after dark, watching more and more logs being driven into the bay. The rain had stopped, but the wind still howled like a pack of wolves bent on doing harm. The moon shone through rifts torn in the clouds, lighting up the bay with a weird glow. The wind blew and the sea raged all the next day.

Chapter Nine

AFTER THE STORM

"I DO hope the wind will drop and the sea go calm before school begins," Geoff told Michael. "You can't think what fun we'll have running out on the logs. They're used as firewood, you know. Last year we had started school before there was a storm from the east, and we had only the evenings free and it got dark quite early. It was the very end of September, you see."

The members of the Valiant Club came home in the next few days and all the boys and girls of the bay chummed up. They couldn't help talking to even those who weren't friends as they watched the logs.

"I'm going to mark that one for Dad," Stubby declared. "Do you see which I mean? It's a beauty."

"No fear, *I'll* get there first," said Geoff laughing. They were all good-tempered about marking the logs: it was part of the game. If they were not the first to reach one that they thought specially good, there would be another. Michael and Rosemary were going to mark logs for the Flynns because Mr. Lansdowne did not need wood. He was sent wood from the firm's timber-yard ready sawn.

Two days after the fateful picnic, everyone woke to find the sun shining and the sky cloudless. There was not even a light breeze. All was still and the sea without a wave. The bay was an amazing sight. The logs had squeezed themselves in together, making a platform stretching two hundred yards out.

Mr. Flynn and Mr. Lansdowne went on to the beach before they left for the city. There was no room to stand on the beach itself, for the logs were close up to the cliffs, so they climbed on to a big log.

"Yes, come along," they called to their children waiting on the road above. "Now, listen," said Mr. Flynn. "You may go out as far as that huge log, that rather short, very fat one that is a bit cocked up. Do you see? But you may not go beyond it."

There may have been twenty yards of loosely-framed logs beyond.

"You understand, don't you? And if the sea should get at all rough again you mustn't climb out at all—but we're pretty sure that it won't."

What a morning of fun they had! They soon tired of painting initials on logs, and after all they did not really know which would burn well and make the best fires. Their dads would have to settle which they would have in the end. So they carried their cans of paint and their brushes up on to the road and arranged a relay race. The logs were dry on their upper sides and the children were barefoot or wearing rubber-soled shoes, so they were able to spring from one log to another safely.

Geoff and Mark Leyton, a boy from Oak Bay about Geoff's age, were chosen to pick sides. There were seven children in each team. The race started from a big log close to the cliff and they had to run to the cocked-up log beyond which they were not to go, and back to the cliff.

It was hard going, for sometimes runners slipped to their knees and had to scramble up while the other team were getting ahead. After eight races with rests in between they were four all. At that moment Mrs. Lansdowne came along the road to tell Michael and Rosemary that it was nearly dinner-time.

"Dinner-time!" the children all exclaimed. The morning seemed to have flown.

"Yes, it's half-past twelve," she told them.

"May we have one more race to settle it?" Geoff asked. "Please let us."

Mrs. Lansdowne couldn't refuse and it was fun watching. However did they leap along so surely and quickly? She was glad that she did not have to join the race. Mark Leyton's team won, and there was cheering.

"Jolly fine your team are," Geoff said. "We challenge you for a return this afternoon. You will have another go, won't you?"

Stubby was in Mark's team and was very proud of their win, but in spite of this he did not feel that he had won his old place among the boys back again. The boys had not quite forgotten how meanly he had treated Michael when he was a newcomer, and how he had bullied him at school, so he was determined to show them that he was really a fine chap as good as anyone, and marking logs would, he thought, give him a chance.

Stubby hurried over his dinner. He must be out first and have a look at the logs beyond the place to which most of the kids were allowed to go by their dads. Of course it was quite different for *him*. His dad had taken him out to where the logs were heaved about when there was a chance wave since the time he was five years old. Stubby forgot in his eagerness that he had never let him go out alone.

He made the climb to a huge cedar log beyond the place where they were jammed together and steady for walking across. He had to jump a few feet to reach it.

Just wait till they saw him away out there! He could have marked the log and just told the other chaps about it, but they wouldn't be able to see the marks from the log jam, and they might just laugh at him and say he was bragging and that he hadn't really been out there at all.

He wished the others would come. He hated waiting. He returned to the beach, ready to start back as soon as enough of them were there to see him. At last Rosemary, Michael and Geoff came along together and he saw Mark and some others in the distance. They would be at the shore by the time he reached the log and see him standing on it. That would show them! He had better set off, for he did not want them to guess that he was waiting for them. They would say he was showing off and of course he really was, but why shouldn't he? He was much the pluckiest of all the boys. He'd prove it.

Directly Rosemary, Michael and Geoff reached the beach, he started. It was easy going as far as the cocked-up log beyond which the other children had been forbidden to go, and Geoff paid little heed to Stubby at first, but when he saw him springing farther out he was alarmed, for the logs were not close together, and Stubby had to leap from one to the next.

"Hi! Look at Stubby!" Geoff exclaimed to Michael and Rosemary. "What does the silly ass think he's doing?"

Mark and his friends were strolling along in the warm afternoon sunshine and weren't looking. Stubby reached the cedar log and stooped down to paint it. At that moment a wave from far out, caused by the wash of a big liner bound for Japan, rode in and lifted the log on which Stubby was standing as if it were a plaything. Stubby was pitched backwards and disappeared between the cedar log and the others tossing a few feet from it. Then the logs closed up over him.

Geoff yelled to Mark, "Go for help." Then he caught hold of Michael. "Come along," he said, "we must get him out. Rosemary, go and tell the Flynns. Quick!"

The two boys ran and jumped faster than in the relay race. Stubby had not appeared again. Geoff was expecting him to appear on the sea side of the cedar log—he should have swum out from underneath. He ought to be up and floating by now, even if he had been hurt and could not swim much. Geoff and Michael reached the cedar log.

"I'm diving in and going to swim under the logs a bit. If I don't get him and can't stay down any longer I'll call you. Come in when I shout."

Michael stood trembling on the cedar log. Then the thought of what Mr. Chisholm had told him flashed into his mind. He prayed as hard and as fast as he could.

"Please let us get Stubby out. Please make me braver than I am."

Praying stopped his legs trembling. Geoff shouted. In Michael went and swam under the logs to the right of the place Geoff had been searching. He managed to keep his eyes open, but at first all seemed black darkness and it was freezing cold. Then he saw light between the cracks, and a gleam of light showed him Stubby's white shirt. He got hold of it and of Stubby. He was heavy, but he didn't struggle. Michael turned on his back and tried to tow him out, but he couldn't find the way. He hadn't much breath left.

"Oh God, do something. I can't do much more," he was praying, when brilliant light nearly blinded him. They were out. Then something hit him on the leg. What happened next he was never sure. He was not certain about anything till he asked, "Where am I?" and a nurse leant over him and said, "You're in an ambulance. Rosemary's here with you. We're taking you to hospital. Is your leg hurting badly?"

Then things were all muddled again, till he woke in bed in the children's ward and his mother and father were there and looking happy.

"We're proud of you, Michael," his father said.

"Where's Geoff? Where's Stubby?" he asked, as things began to come back to him, and he remembered getting hold of Stubby underneath those horrible logs.

"Stubby's all right and so is Geoff. They had to work on Stubby a while. He'd drunk a lot of water. Geoff only got a cut, not a bad one."

"What have I got? My leg aches."

"A broken leg. It was caught between two logs, but it's a clean break and well set. It's in plaster now. It won't go on hurting for long, the surgeon says, and you will be coming home in a day or two. But when your leg aches remember how proud we are of you. You saved Stubby's life. Geoff couldn't have managed alone."

The next day Mr. Chisholm visited Michael. He brought him the parts of a model yacht to put together. They had a talk about Stubby. "You'll be friends now, I know. It's horrid not to feel friends with people, isn't it? I am proud of you, Michael."

"I'm awfully afraid I'll get swelled head."

"Oh no, you won't! People don't if they're afraid of getting it. God doesn't let them."

"It was God who made me able to see Stubby and stopped my legs trembling. I prayed like you told me to."

"Shall I help you to start the yacht?" Mr. Chisholm suggested. They were at it when a nurse told them

Stubby had come to see Michael. He was glad Mr. Chisholm was there.

"Don't go, please don't go!" Michael begged when he heard Stubby was coming.

"Come along and help us with this," Mr. Chisholm said as Stubby was shown in, but Stubby was determined to say what he had planned.

"Michael, you're an awfully fine, brave chap. I can't say thank you properly ever. I can't, really."

"Michael knows what you mean," Mr. Chisholm helped him out.

"Michael, please be a member of the Valiants Club. Please do. We all want you ever so."

"Oh, how *spiffling*! I'd love to be, and I never thought I would. Thanks awfully, Stubby."

For ten minutes or so Mr. Chisholm stayed and the three worked on the yacht together and then Stubby left.

"It's funny," Mr. Chisholm said teasingly, "but I always heard that boasting was your trouble. Now you've done something really worth talking about——"

"And I just feel humble. I never knew before what it was *really* like—to be a pilgrim. But I'm starting now."